PIGLOO

Anne Marie Pace

Illustrated by Lorna Hussey

SCHOLASTIC INC.

ISBN 978-1-338-16295-0

12 11 10 9 8 7 6 5 4 3 2   17 18 19 20 21 22

Printed in the U.S.A.   40

First Scholastic printing, January 2017

Designed by Liz Dresner
The illustrations for this book were created with watercolor and graphite.

For Mom and Dad, who made the hot chocolate
—A. M. P.

For my dearest friends
Dawn, Nicky, Lynn, Kerry, Elaine, and little Sheila
with all my love
—L. H.

Pigloo is an explorer. He is destined for greatness and glory. He is planning an expedition to the North Pole.

Pigloo has a new sled. He has the
boots and mittens and hat that his
mother will make him wear.

He has stores (that's what explorers
call snacks) in his backpack.
But Pigloo must wait for the snow.

His father says, "Sometimes great explorers must
be patient as well as brave."

(That is the sort of thing fathers of explorers say.)

Paisley says, "Pigloo does not know how to be patient *or* brave."

(That is the sort of thing big sisters of explorers say.)

Pigloo ignores her and practices
driving his dogsled.

Finally, one evening the first
flakes fall.

Pigloo grabs his boots and mittens and hat.

Paisley says, "If you go outside now, you'll be exploring in mud."

Pigloo likes mud, but he will like snow better.

From his dogsled,
Pigloo searches for the
North Star. Even with
his spyglass, he cannot
find it through the
flurries.

In the morning, Pigloo puts on his boots and mittens and hat. His mother tells him to take off his hat to eat his eggs. (Hats at the table are the sort of thing mothers of explorers don't like.)

"Are you going sledding today?" she asks.

"I am going to the North Pole," Pigloo says. "With Paisley."

"You know Admiral Byrd already found it, right?" Paisley asks.
"And I'm not going."

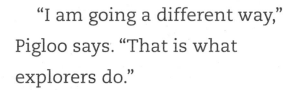

"I am going a different way," Pigloo says. "That is what explorers do."

"And how will you know when you get there?" his father asks.

"When I see the red-and-white-striped pole," Pigloo says. "And maybe a polar bear."

Outside, Pigloo considers the best way to get
to the North Pole and back before lunch.
    Finding north is easy, but breaking through
the snow is hard.

Pigloo needs a faster way to travel.
Sledding down a hill will give him all
the speed he needs.

But at the top of the hill, Pigloo
realizes that the hill isn't just
big—it's huge.

He dawdles and delays. It is a
very,

very,

very

huge

hill.

But sledding is the only way to get to the North Pole and back before lunch. Pigloo does not need his father or his mother to remind him that great explorers need to be brave. And he really doesn't need to know what Paisley might say.

Pigloo takes a deep breath and
throws himself onto his sled.
He swoops past bushes and trees.
He shoots over bumps and dips.
His stomach flips and flops.

Snow flies everywhere, but Pigloo keeps his eyes open so he'll know when he's found the North Pole.

Just ahead, in the great expanse of white, Pigloo sees a flash of red. Could it be . . . ? It is!

He rams his boots into the snow and pulls the rope until he stops.

There's a red-and-white-striped pole.
And a polar bear.
And part of an igloo.
And Paisley.

"You said you weren't coming," Pigloo reminds her.

"I came a different way," she says. "The short way."

"I didn't know there was a short way," Pigloo says.

"Now you do," Paisley says. "Let's finish the igloo."

Because Paisley knows the
short way, it does not take
nearly as long to get home.

Inside, his mother hands him a mug of hot
chocolate and a bowl of tomato soup.

(That is the sort of food mothers want
explorers to eat when they are cold.)

"So," his father says, "how was the North Pole?"

"Good," Pigloo says. He swallows his last sip of hot chocolate. "But there were no penguins."

"Not at the North Pole," Paisley says. "Penguins only live at the South Pole."

"I like penguins. I think I'll try for the South Pole before supper," Pigloo says.

Paisley already has her coat on.

"Paisley is coming," Pigloo announces happily.

"Aren't you?"

Paisley grabs her boots and mittens
and hat. And her backpack, full of stores.
"I am," she says.

"Somebody has to show you the short way."